W. Phillpotts Williams

Rhymes in Red

W. Phillpotts Williams

Rhymes in Red

ISBN/EAN: 9783337264147

Printed in Europe, USA, Canada, Australia, Japan

Cover: Foto ©Andreas Hilbeck / pixelio.de

More available books at **www.hansebooks.com**

RHYMES IN RED

BY

W. PHILLPOTTS WILLIAMS

FORMERLY MASTER AND HUNTSMAN OF THE NETTON HARRIERS
AUTHOR OF "POEMS IN PINK" "PLAIN POEMS"
AND "OVER THE OPEN"

WITH 51 ILLUSTRATIONS BY CUTHBERT BRADLEY

SALISBURY: BROWN & CO.
LONDON
SIMPKIN, MARSHALL, HAMILTON, KENT & CO. LTD.
1899

The poems marked * have already appeared in "Plain Poems," and those marked † in "Baily's Magazine," from which they have been reprinted with permission. The rest are entirely new.

CONTENTS.

—◆◆—

* RIDE FOR DEAR LIFE.

OVER the moorland the daylight is creeping,
  Dimly the dawn has crept over the hill ;
Somebody whispers while others are weeping,
  "Quick, for God's sake, she is dangerously ill.

"Ride for the doctor, go round to the stable,
  Take the brown mare, you must ride for dear life,
Trust to her speed, she is willing and able,
  Haste, you must save her, your beautiful wife."

Moving mechanically, meekly obeying,
  Yonder the bridle, the bit and bredoon ;
Now to the stable, the good mare is neighing,
  Come to the door, there is light from the moon.

Over the moorland, away we are speeding,
  Over the moorland we gallantly fly,
Quickly the mare shows the worth of her breeding,
  Ride for dear life, or our darling will die.

B

Furlong by furlong we throw them behind us,
　　Stroke upon stroke with her wonderful stride :
Not a pulsation but seems to remind us
　　Life may depend on this desperate ride.

Furlong by furlong, still beating the measure,
　　Foam on the bridle and sweat on the rein,
Ever before me the face of my treasure—
　　God ! shall I never caress her again ?

Over the granite we go with a rattle,
　　Up the steep pathway, and down the decline,
On by the herd of the terrified cattle,
　　Over the moorland we keep to the line.

Locked ! it is strange, see the gateway is standing
　　There where the roadway is rugged and steep ;
Bad the take off, and indifferent the landing,
　　A bar on the top, it's a desperate leap.

Rouse ye, my bonny steed, neatly collecting
　　All your strong quarters beneath for a spring,
Thoughts of the danger our senses infecting,
　　Life may depend on your stride and your swing.

Straight for the gate, will she turn ? never fear it,
　　Neatly she judges it, gamely she tries ;
Is it too much for her ? now ! will she clear it ?
　　Up to it, close to it, *over* she flies.

Gratefully touching her neck, I caress her,
  Words cannot utter my feelings to-day ;
Over the moorland again do I press her,
  On to the hamlet that sleeps by the bay.

          *   *   *   *   *

The crisis is over, and twilight is stealing
  Over the valley and over the hill ;
Down by the side of my wife I am kneeling,
  Hush ! for her slumbers are peaceful and still.

Angels are guarding her, silently sleeping.
  Angels are watching her beautiful face ;
Over the moorland the sunset is creeping,
  Nature reposes with exquisite grace.

Silently, silently, sunbeams are falling,
  Brightly they light every wave of her hair :
Softly the voices of nature are calling,
  Sounds of sweet sympathy float on the air.

Softly, oh, night wind thy way thou art wending
  Over the moorland and over the sea ;
On to the regions above thou art tending,
  Bear on thy bosom a message from me.

Tell of our love to the Maker who gave us
  Life reunited again for a spell,
Tell of the steed who was willing to save us,
  Tell of our gratitude, faithfully tell,

How in our love we are welded together,
   Sacred the promise, and solemn the tie :
How, when we come to the end of our tether,
   Still in that love we are willing to die.

BLOOD WILL TELL.

BLOOD WILL TELL.

COME, bear with me, reader, and pause for awhile ;
   A tale of the chase I will tell.
"That subject again ? " Yes, I thought you would smile :
But it's all I'm allowed, for the critics revile
   If I try to take others as well.

Perhaps, after all, it's a gain in the end
   To be tied to the subject you love.
And when you have taken the horse as a friend
Through trouble and care, you're prepared to defend
   Him, as something sent down from above.

But hark ! in the spinney, the hounds are away ;
  A cap is held high in the air ;
The man on the brown and the man on the grey
Are over the fence, they are riding to-day,
  And free as the birds in the air.

And mark in the meadow, the mare and the foal
  Are stirred by the musical cry.
My word ! what a sort ; see, she stands on the knoll—
The sound of the music is rousing her soul—
  The old mare is eager to fly.

But there ! look at that : she is over the fence—
  She takes the whole thing at a bound.
And look at the foal, he has scarcely the sense—
He has, though ; well done ! see, his stride is immense,
  His quarters are massive and round.

Away, yes, away, through the heart of the vale
  The old mare is leading the field.
She notes the good hounds as they gallantly sail,
And tackles the blackthorn, and tackles the rail ;
  She was always too plucky to yield.

And look at the foal, ever close in her wake
  The young one is true to the breed.
He judges his distance, and knows how to take
Off, just in the right place, and lands with a shake
  Of the head that shows courage and speed.

The stile in the corner, the ditch, and the drop,
　　It pounds both the brown and the grey ;
But the mare steadies down, with a lurch and a lop,
And both old one and young one go over it—pop !
　　Then forrard, still forrard away.

See, there in the bank they have marked him to ground,
　　This fox that made everyone ride.
The mare, who has led from the time that we found,
Is cropping the grass, with the hounds grouped around,
　　With the bonny foal close to her side.

Three cheers for the science ! Three cheers for the chase !
　　The hounds that ne'er falter or tire ;
Three cheers for the cattle that join in the race,
The young and the old, with such exquisite grace,
　　And the music that fills them with fire.

And now, gentle reader, good-night, and farewell :
　　We've ridden the run to the end.
The soft winter sunlight is lighting the dell,
And, journeying homewards, we talk and we tell
　　How each sportsman is counted a friend.

And long may it prosper, this pastime so fair,
　　The chase that we cherish so dear.
Through the heart of the vale in the silvery air
May we still ride away from all trouble and care,
　　With the hounds flying on to the cheer.

THE YOUNG HUSSAR.

THE YOUNG HUSSAR.

"Halt !" is the order to squadrons advancing,
    "Dress by your right and dismount, the brigade."
See, on the sabres the sunlight is dancing ;
    "Loosen your girths, get the men in the shade."

Yonder an aid-de-camp, dashing and striding,
    Orders direct from the staff, it would seem
Something important ; how fast he is riding
    Up to the Colonel, who stands by the stream.

Some special service ; yes, hark ! they are seeking
    For someone to volunteer now for the work.
Listen !—the issue is vital ; they're speaking,
    Asking for someone who'll ride, and not shirk.

Maps of the country, with much information,
    Important despatches for those in command
Of the army's left wing ; there will be consternation
    If they should fail to be carried by hand.

Yonder a subaltern gracefully standing,
    Offering his services, faithful and true.
Yonder he stands by the Colonel commanding,
    Asking for work he is willing to do.

Fair are his features, and youthful his bearing ;
    The pet of the regiment, the favourite at home ;
One with a manner and way so endearing,
    One whose young life tells of pleasures to come.

Mark the dark chestnut impatiently stamping—
    Hermit's great grandson, and true to his sire—
Pricking his ears at the infantry tramping,
    Raising his head, full of courage and fire.

Now they are off.   See, the rider is seated
    Easy and light, as a child in his chair,
Passing his troop, where he's cheerily greeted—
    Forward the light dragoon, faithful and fair.

Right through the enemy's lines he is riding,
　　Up the wide valley, and over the hill ;
Faster and faster the chestnut is striding ;
　　Faster.   The good horse is galloping still.

Faster.   The tents of the left wing are gleaming
　　Hard by the verge of the silvery sea.
Faster.   The chestnut's dark quarters are streaming.
　　Faster and faster, and faithful and free.

All is accomplished, the maps and despatches
　　Both are delivered with quickness and care.
Pausing a moment the subaltern snatches
　　Some food, which the rider and bonny steed share.

Then in the twilight the chestnut is sailing
　　Back with his master to join the brigade.
Hark ! there's a shot ! and a cry !   Is he ailing?
　　Look at the subaltern there in the shade.

Down on the ground by the trees he is lying ;
　　Fatal the bullet and fatal its course.
Yonder the outpost that spied him still flying
　　On like a bird on his dark chestnut horse.

Then, in a moment, sweet memories come o'er him :
　　Thoughts of his home by the side of the Dee ;
Forms of the dear ones he knew move before him,
　　Calling him back to them over the lea.

Wandering through the old paths, he is treading
  Still in the footsteps he trod as a child ;
Clearer and clearer the picture is spreading,
  Clearer the landscape, and graceful and wild.

Now in the church in the park he is kneeling
  As in his childhood, and learning to pray ;
Placing his hand in his mother's, and feeling
  Some of her influence lighting the way.

Softly, still softly and sweetly, she leads him ;
  Hush ! her sweet influence guides him in death.
She, who has passed its dark portal, still needs him :
  Dear to her now as he breathes his last breath.

    *   *   *   *   *

Still is the night where the watch-fires are gleaming,
  Sleeping the men of the gallant brigade ;
Still is the glen where the moonlight is streaming ;
  Still are the horses that stand in the shade.

Hush ! there's a neigh on the flank, and a tremble,
  As a riderless horse joins his comrades again.
A bonny dark chestnut—no need to dissemble—
  The hand of his rider is still on the plain.

A COUNTRY DRIVE.

A COUNTRY DRIVE.

Put the rein at cheek and let her
Go ; now steady, do not fret her.
Take the sheet from off her quarter, she is all alive to-day.
Yes, we know the way to travel
As we glide along the gravel,
When the dark grey mare is stepping, stepping, stepping all
the way.

See, her silver mane is flowing
And her glossy coat is glowing,
Glowing, glowing in the sunlight as it streams across the
vale.

And the fresh breeze in our faces
Passes by us as it races
With the snow-white clouds above us—oh, how peacefully
      they sail.

Sailing on we beat the measure
While the footsteps of my treasure
Blend in concord with the morning, making music bright
      and gay ;
And the great dark trees above us
Bend and move and seem to love us,
While the dark grey mare is stepping, stepping, stepping all
      the way.

Now a reverence comes o'er me
As the scene stands out before me,
And the wide and spreading landscape tells of England far
      and wide ;
And the mist is rising lightly
Through the light that shines so brightly
On the cottage homes that spread themselves about the
      country-side.

Then we cross the shining river
Where the lights and sunbeams quiver,
And the old stone bridge re-echoes 'neath the hoof-strokes
      of the grey.

And the winding road before us
Seems to mingle with the chorus,
While the dark grey mare is stepping, stepping, stepping all
    the way.

Then old memories come, and waking,
Tell of when my heart was breaking,
And my mind goes drifting sadly to the years long, long
    ago ;
And a fair form seems to meet me
By the old grey house, and greet me
As it did when I was younger, in the years long, long ago.

Then it comes, that sacred feeling,
And those nights that found me kneeling,
And the dark, dark time of torture, and the breaking of
    the day ;
And my sad thoughts seem to mingle
With the scene, and senses tingle,
While the dark grey mare is stepping, stepping, stepping all
    the way.

After, when the moon is shining
And the day is fast declining,
And the object of my journey is accomplished, I return.
In the wood the shades are falling,
Where the lonely owl is calling,
And the herd of timid deer are lying hidden in the fern.

Later on, when I am dreaming
And the silver meads are gleaming,
Still the flying wheels beneath me make a music bright and
　　gay ;
And a thrill of life comes o'er me
As I see the road before me,
While the dark grey mare is stepping, stepping, stepping all
　　the way.

RANTER

CUTHBERT BRADLEY

"THE PETERBOROUGH VERDICT."

RANTER.

"You'll walk us a pup? I'll be glad if you will,"
The huntsman called out, as he drove up the hill.
"I know you're a sportsman, and courteous, and kind,
And will help us to make up the pack—do you mind?"

"A puppy?" I said, looking up with a smile,
While I thought of the ducklings and turkeys the while.
"Oh, come ; yes you will," said the huntsman again,
And then he discovered my wife in the lane ;

At which he took off his new hat, with a bow,
And asked for the pigs and the Alderney cow.
He said she looked young for her age, did my wife,
Her figure was wonderful, too, for her life.

Well, so it was settled : my wife with a laugh
Said she was not the one to be caught with such chaff :
But she asked him inside the farmhouse all the same.
And gave him some ale, and was pleased that he came.

The puppy became quite at home the first day ;
He looked upon life as a joke, and the way
He treated each action that came as a part
Of a great entertainment, made after his heart,

Was comical to a degree. But the sight
Was to see him go round the farmyard the first night :
He went for the ducks with a leap and a bound,
Falling head over heels on the side of the mound :

And then he discovered an elderly sow
Fast asleep on her side (we expected a row).
How quaintly he moved, and how gingerly, too :
He crept to her back, which quite hid him from view.

He sniffed the whole way till he came to her ear,
Which he touched with his paw, but it filled him with fear
When it moved, and he thought 'twould be best to retire
And watch from a distance, so paused to admire.

But this was too much for our friend, 'twould appear,
For he ran in again, and sniffed hard at the ear ;
At this the old lady got up in a rage
And, thinking him forward, no doubt, for his age,

Made a rush at the pup with her snout in the air,
Which made him run up the long lane like a hare.
The next day being Sunday, this man of research
Got into the dairy when we were at church ;

And when we returned, he was covered with cream,
Which was running away from his neck in a stream.
He welcomed us gladly, and seemed quite delighted,
As though we were guests, and expressly invited.

The air of good nature he wore, and the way
He showed us about was as good as a play ;
And then, after dinner we found him asleep
In the bedroom upstairs, where he lay in a heap

On the bed, which he covered with patches of dirt :
His pillow, we found, was my latest new shirt.
And after a while, he grew into a hound,
And stood like a monarch, and covered the ground.

A play of the shoulder, a strength of the back,
With bone to the feet that fell firm on the track.
Oh, yes, I believe you, he thrived and did well,
This hound that we reared at the farm in the dell.

When, later, the puppy-show came, it was clear
That Ranter would be the best hound of the year.
The judges soon spotted this gem of the casket,
And gave him the prize as the pick of the basket.

And well I remember that cub-hunting morn,
When the daylight came up with the first streak of dawn :
When the hounds in the covert were eager and keen,
And spoke to the line where their quarry had been.

How Ranter went off on the line of a hare,
" Baik gently then, Ranter boy. Baik ! have a care."
And after he entered and ran like a man,
Running up with the best in his place in the van.

And after the hunting was over there came
A time when good Ranter was covered with fame ;
For the Peterborough verdict was " special and cup "
For the hound that we reared at the farm as a pup.

And now the whole kennel is full of his strain,
The whole of them hunt in the drought or the rain ;
And Ranter himself, after seasons of work,
In which the hound never attempted to shirk,

Has come to the farm to repose at his ease,
And where you may see him to-day, if you please,
Stretched out by the grate, quite contented, it seems,
For the old hound is hunting the fox in his dreams.

"A FRANTIC RUSH, WITH A KNIFE IN HAND."

TOM BLAKE AND THE DAPPLED BROWN.

WHAT, yonder grave? Did you know Tom Blake?
    The man who could ride the vale.
The first to ride from the waving brake,
    The last to give hounds a hail.

I knew him well, he was born near here :
    Tom Blake was a farmer's son ;
The good brown nag that he held so dear
    He bred, 'twas a real good one.

I see them still in my fancy's eye,
   Tom Blake and the dappled brown
The man could ride and the horse could fly,
   And yet they were seldom down.   .

I see him still, as he faced the brook
   Where the stream was deep and wide ;
The whole field turned with a frightened look,
   But Tom would not be denied.

Away, away, they were riding still,
   Away through the silver air.
They faced the vale, and they faced the hill,
   But none could get near the pair.

Another day in the farmers' race,
   When the hunt gave a point to point,
They pulled it off at a rattling pace.
   The rest were put out of joint.

The mare was tame as a cat, they said,
   And followed Tom up and down.
The bond of love was strong, they said,
   'Twixt Tom and the dappled brown.

And once we saw, when the night was bright,
   A flare in the midnight sky :
A column of smoke, and a ruddy light
   At the farm, it soon caught the eye.

But Tom had gone to the town that day,
    And locked the strong stable door.
The roof had caught, and was giving way
    As well as the old loft floor.

A cry went up, and a passing thrill
    As they thought of the dappled brown ;
She was tied with a rope to the manger still -
    Good God ! would the floor come down ?

But help, a-hoy ! take a beam, my lads,
    And stave in the stable door.
Once more, a-hoy ! —take a run, my lads—
    Are you ready ? —now—once more

The door gives way as a man appears,
    'Tis Tom, now returned from town ;
We tell the tale of our hopes and fears
    And point to the dappled brown.

We point the hand to the falling beams,
    And say he must lose the horse ;
But Tom will not hear of that, it seems,
    And decides on another course.

A frantic rush, with a knife in hand,
    And Tom cuts through the rope ;
And the brown horse struggles to where we stand.
    Hurrah !—we are filled with hope.

But a crashing noise, and a piercing cry
    Fills every man's heart with fear ;
And the black smoke floats through the midnight sky
    As we pause for awhile to hear.

We dragged him forth from beneath the wreck,
    A crushed and a mangled form.
We looked, and found there was still a speck
    Of life that survived the storm.

But the speck was faint, and he breathed his last
    In the yard, where we laid him down ;
And the only words from his lips that passed
    Were, "Thank God, I have saved the brown."

And the good mare, too, when she saw him there—
    The man she had known so well —
Sniffed hard at the face and the matted hair,
    With a snort at the smoky smell.

So now good-night ; look across the vale,
    The sun is behind the down.
That's all I know, 'tis a well-known tale,
    Tom Blake and the dappled brown.

THE RANCHMAN'S VISION OF HOME.

THE RED ROAN MARE.

He laid his hand on the red roan mare
   And looked at her shapely side ;
He saw her eye, which was bright and fair,
   And thought of her dashing stride.

Away, away, o'er the lonely down,
   To the arch of the sinking sky ;
To the flaming lights of the village town —
   My word ! how the mare can fly.

He thought him then of his own career,
   The illness that wrecked his life :
The fair young face that he held so dear,
   Who now was another's wife.

He thought him then of what might have been,
   Of the home with its children sweet ;
And then he turned to another scene,
   His life, on its lonely beat.

So on he rode on the red roan mare,
   His heart beating quick and fast :
As true as steel, and as light as air,
   The mare she could go and last.

But softly now 'neath the thick thorn hedge,
   And stand by the old oak tree ;
Where the peaceful house on the lawn-set ledge
   Looks out on the sloping lea.

For there through a window that opens wide
   A group by the lamplight shows ;
The husband posed by his fair young bride,
   While the young child laughs and crows.

" One long last look," said the horseman bold,
   As he sat on the red roan mare.
" One long, last look, ere my heart grows cold
   Ah, God ! what a scene is there."

"God help them, yet," said the horseman bold.
    Who thought of the sacred fire
That kindled the hearts of the group, and told
    Of love that can never tire.

And back he rode through the village town,
    His tears coming thick and fast ;
Away, away, o'er the lonely down
    Where the night wind rushes past.

And later on, and across the seas,
    Alone, on a Texas ranch,
A horseman lies 'neath the stately trees,
    Beneath a great spreading branch ;

And tethered near is a red roan mare,
    A friend ever staunch and true ;
Around them both is the soft night air,
    Where the white mist passes through.

And far away, so the horseman dreams,
    In the land he loves so well,
A fair young wife, bending down, it seems.
    O'er a child in a shady dell.

And a prayer goes up from a lonely heart.
    A prayer and a stifled cry.
God help them, yet may they play their part,
    Man has but to live and die.

THE OLD SORT.

THE OLD SORT.

I'll give you a sportsman, a man, and a friend,
   A nailer to handle the horn ;
A man one was always prepared to defend,
Whose friendship was strong, and endured to the end
   A truer man never was born.

A picture he was, as he sat on his horse :
   His features were handsome and strong ;
His bushy grey eyebrows and hair added force
To his face, while his eye looked on life and its course
   With a keenness both lasting and long.

His dress was old-fashioned, it suited him well,
   A broad-brimmed flat hat, and a tie
That went twice round his throat –he was never a swell
While his green hunting frock was made neatly, and fell
   Well over his muscular thigh.

And what of the hunter, and what of the brown ?
   A cart horse in make and in frame ;
Three parts thoroughbred—do you doubt it, look down
At his tapering thighs, then look up at his crown -
   You can see he's a blood one, and game.

Now look at the hounds ; they're an old-fashioned kind.
   Blue mottled and long in the ear ;
All bred to a type, and so sorty, you'll find
A family likeness in all that should bind
   Them close in a working career.

But come, gentle reader, come out to the hills ;
   Come, lend me yourself for awhile ;
I'll take you away from all worries and ills.
Mark the sportsman in question, his face how it fills
   With pleasure ; take note of his smile.

Just hark at him, now ; there's a rattling cheer;
   He waves his hounds into the heather.
They're spreading about ; there's a hare, never fear :
Look, yonder she goes, 'neath the gate ; look and near
   Are the hounds running, facing the weather.

And forrard again—how they twist and they turn
   As over the valley they fly ;
Each hound is at work, and is anxious to learn
The way of his hare, and is quick to discern
   The line on the stubble, " Yut try."

And mark how they check in the wind and the rain ;
   They're feathering away with a will.
See them spreading and casting again and again,
And it's " Hark to it, Primula, over the lane,"
   The hare has turned under the hill.

But mark the old sort, see his workmanlike seat ;
   He sits like a centaur, I vow.
He lets them alone, for he thinks it a treat
To see hounds at work by themselves. " Mind the wheat !
   Ride round, and go over the plough."

Look, look ! he has viewed her, the farmer in brown,
   His hat is held high in the air.
Don't holloa, they're hunting it over the down ;
See, Rarity catches a view on the crown
   Of the hill.   It's who-whoop ! I declare.

And so have I seen him, this sportsman and friend,
   Before he was laid in the soil ;
His friendship will influence me still to the end,
And the force of his cheery example will tend
   To guide me through trouble and toil.

Oh, what is the secret contained in the chase
   That knits men so firmly, and binds
Them closely together ; and lends them such grace
In all things pertaining to hunting?   The base
   Of hunting is kindness : it finds

Us out at each point, and each turn of the game :
   The farmer who lends us the land ;
The owners of coverts, with them it's the same —
One courtesy runs through the whole, and the aim
   Is to form an harmonious band.

And what of the hunter, and what of the hound
   So noble, so gentle, and true ?
'Tis kindness directs every action and bound ;
While the cheer of the huntsman, that musical sound,
   Has a ring of true sympathy too.

And such was our friendship —we knew not of strife :
   A friendship both firm and sincere ;
It comes to me still, when the moments are rife
With action in chase—still he rides as in life,
   With his hounds flying on to the cheer.

WITH THE QUEEN'S STAGHOUNDS.

A SCENE IN ENGLAND.

YONDER lies the place of meeting,
Where each sportsman finds a greeting.
Yonder goes the stag uncarted, stepping lightly all the way,
And the merry chase is sailing
By the dim and distant paling ;
While the horn is sounding sweetly, making music bright
and gay.

Then a softer stillness follows
When the distant horn and holloas

Die away beyond the hillside, and the chase is fleeting far :
    And a calmer mood comes o'er me
    As I watch the scene before me,
And I look on smiling England, and the peaceful things
      that are.

    There I see her sweetly spreading
    Where the zephyr wind is heading
On towards the smoking hamlet, with the river winding by :
    And the peaceful scene appealing
    Stirs my heart with love and feeling
For the land we love so dearly, and the cause we count so
      high.

    As I think, I see her moving
    Forward, forward still, and proving
All the strength of her great purpose, and her fight for
      freedom still ;
    And the golden sunlight falling
    Augurs brightly for her calling,
While the distant horn is sounding far away behind the hill.

    Then I look, and think, and ponder,
    And my mind goes drifting yonder,
Where the stately heights of Windsor stand so bright against
      the sky ;
    And the royal standard floating
    Waves its soft silk folds, denoting
How the great illustrious Lady holds her Court with dignity.

So my heart is stirred with feeling
As the silver light is stealing
On the stately towers and battlements that meet me as I
    gaze ;
And the future years seem brighter
For the good Queen's work, and lighter
Seems the struggle for existence in the dark and crowded
    ways.

Then I turn my steps, ascending
Where the dusky road is bending ;
And I loiter on the causeway, where I ponder for awhile ;
And I hear a "Gently, Speedy,"
As the hounds, so smart and breedy,
Come upon me in the twilight as I stand beside the stile.

Fainter, fainter, I can hear them,
With the horsemen jogging near them.
Fainter, fainter is the music of their feet upon the way :
And my better heart rejoices
As I hear those merry voices
As they join in bright discussion on the merits of the day.

So it goes, and softly creeping
Fall the shadows on the sleeping

Hamlet, where the lights are burning, and the music of the
        night
    Wraps the whole in sweet composure ;
    And across the wide enclosure
Drifts the white night mist, that, rising, passes onwards on
        its flight.

THE SUITORS THREE.

THE SUITORS THREE.

Away in the vale, where the meadows were gleaming,
   A fair lady rider was leading the chase ;
Out over the brook, where the waters were streaming,
   She rode with decision and exquisite grace.

And hard in her wake were three suitors contending
    Each one for a place by her side as she raced ;
Three red-coated rivals were quickly descending
    The hill from the covert, but all were outpaced.

And, after awhile, when they checked, one approached her
    Alone, on his words it is useless to dwell ;
He looked at her sadly, 'twould seem, and reproached her :
    " No thank you," she said ; " I love hunting too well."

Another appeared when the chase was completed —
    The fox was at earth—with his story to tell ;
He spoke of his wealth, and he begged and entreated :
    " No thank you," she said ; " I love hunting too well."

And, journeying home, with the shadows reclining,
    The third suitor rode by her side through the dell ;
He pleaded his case, but she smiled and, declining,
    Said, " Thank you, Sir, no ; I love hunting too well."

And she laughed in her sly way, and thought of them
    pleading,
    While she laid her light hand on the neck of the mare :
" I would rather have you, with your courage and breeding,"
    She said, " than a husband and wealth, I declare."

So here's to the cause that she loves, and the holloa
    Which rings through the woodland and floats to the sky :
To the soul-stirring notes of the hounds that we follow,
    The pluck and endurance—the never say die.

Long, long, may it live in the land that we treasure,
   This love of the chase, may it long be our pride ;
And the fair lady rider who counts it a pleasure,
   Long may she be able to gallop and ride.

Forester.

FORESTER.

FORESTER, yes, he is true to his breeding;
 Yonder his picture, it hangs in the hall.
Ah! so you noted him: Forester leading
 Over the open in front of them all.

One of the Belvoir sort, wiry and active,
 Full of good looks, aye, and true to his sire;
Quick in his action, and bright and attractive,
 Forester always has courage and fire.

Come now, I'll tell it you, Forester's story.
   Take the armchair now, and light a cigar.
Yes, it's a pleasure to tell of his glory,
   Though it comes sadly, and comes with a jar.

Forester came from a friend, who has drifted
   Out on the silent and mystical way ;
One with a mind intellectually gifted ;
   One who was fairly well known in his day.

Brought up together from childhood, we started
   Early in life with a friendship that bound
Both into one — it was seldom we parted ;
   Each of us worshipped the note of a hound.

Then, when we grew to an age, we took over
   The whole of the country, each hunted a pack ;
Both were united, and both were in clover,
   Sailing along on the velvety track.

After there came a sad illness, that laid him
   Low in the midst of a brilliant career ;
Sorrow and suffering and pain only made him
   Patienticr, and to his comrades more dear.

Then, on a night when the moonlight was creeping
   Over the silvery breast of the vale,
A group of sad comrades stood round him, and weeping,
   Watched the still face that was peaceful and pale.

Then, when he spoke, he said, " Forester, take him,
  Take the best hound ever cheered to a line ;
Keep him for my sake, and hunt him, and make him
  King of the kennel, for your sake and mine."

So it was Forester came.   It's a pleasure
  To watch him at head, or to guide him to cry ;
But what most delights is the memory I treasure,
  The strong form that lingers so clear in mine eye.

And still as I hear them, the horn and the holloa,
  The stirring sweet music that comes with the chase,
I think of the man I delighted to follow,
  Riding before me with exquisite grace.

Still, in my fancy, his form is beside me ;
  Still is his influence strong in my mind ;
Still his high notions of life seem to guide me,
  Heard through the song of the whispering wind.

Then, as my good horse is beating the measure,
  Strong in the stroke of his wonderful stride,
Every pulsation depicts me my treasure
  Sailing along with the galloping tide.

What is this life, with its mystical ending ?
  Shades of departed friends, where do you dwell ?
Is not your function to guide us, befriending
  Those who in lifetime befriended you well ?

So may I know he is riding beside me
    Up the long hillside and down the decline :
So may his notions of life ever guide me,
    Helping me on as I stick to the line.

That is the whole ; now my story is ended.
    Forester still is a link with the past.
Friendship and Forester gracefully blended
    Hold me to-day, and will hold to the last.

THE POST-BOY'S DREAM.

THE POST-BOY'S DREAM.

Asleep in his chair, the old post-boy is dreaming :
  The dull town and houses have faded away ;
The light of his life is now silently gleaming :
  The scenes of his youth make him happy and gay.

He sees the long vista of roadway inclining
  Away by the river, away to the hill ;
He sees the old Inn, where red creepers are twining
  About the deep porch, and the far distant mill.

And hark !—an excitement—there's someone approaching.
     " A chaise out directly—the chestnut and grey."
The sun is going down, and the twilight's encroaching.
     " Away at a gallop ! Go on, Bill, away ! "

And now he can feel her, the chestnut he's riding,
     The lean neck and quarters, the wonderful stride ;
The game little grey, who is always confiding ;
     A creature in whom it's a treat to confide.

And still he can hear them still beating the measure,
     The roll of the gallop, the hum of the wheels,
The runaway couple inside.   It's a pleasure
     To do them a turn, so he gallops and feels

The old spirit rising within him, and rousing
     The horses who make little count of their load ;
He passes a cluster of yokels carousing,
     Who give him a toast—" The romance of the road."

Then onward again, where the shadows are falling ;
     Then onward again, till they come to the mail,
Which the young couple join, while the guard greets them,
       calling
     Out : " London ? Yes ? Up with you ! "—onward they sail.

And then a confusion of traffic arises
     Before him along the long highway again ;
A varied assortment of sorts and surprises,
     A mixture of vehicles, gaudy and plain.

A waggon of goods, where the horses are straining
    Hard, all at their work, which is stiff it would seem ;
A fast-swinging coach, where the horses are gaining
    On all—"Stand aside ! It's the galloping team."

And all through the valley he sees them, and floating
    The notes of the horn come along the clear air ;
Each one of them silvery, bright, and denoting
    A life of excitement, a progress so fair.

And still the old spirit that stirred him is rising :
    The notes of the horn sound out mellow and clear ;
The music of life is still bright and surprising,
    And everything bids him good luck and good cheer.

But hark ! What is that ? Not the coach and the horses
    That flies by the window. What ! must he confess ?
A railway ! Good God ! Yet his vision endorses
    The fact—it's a vulgar and noisy express.

THE WHITE CHARGER'S STORY.

THE WHITE CHARGER'S STORY.

So you are the clean bred filly that has come to the field
    to stay,
To dwell with the old white charger—a horse who has had
    his day.
My word ! you are a made un, and, like those of your
    kind,
You've the dash of the mountain torrent and the pace of
    the desert wind.

But come, you wild young creature ; come, stand beneath
    the shade,
And hear the charger's story, within yon rustic glade.
Come, rest your limbs beneath you, and hear me while I
    tell
The tale of the Indian Frontier, where the dark-faced
    warriors dwell.

My master, you know, was Colonel, commanding a frontier
    force ;
His men could fight like devils, they called them the Devil's
    Horse ;
And him, their gallant leader, they loved him to a man,
And swore they'd ride to glory when he rode in the van.

Well, once the tribes were rising, the dark-faced warriors
    came
Down from the mountain gorges, those men of fighting
    fame ;
They swarmed about the hillside, they swarmed about the
    vale,
Those dark-faced Indian warriors, so swarthy and so
    hale.

At night we camped below them, beside the lonely stream—
You saw in the gathering darkness the watch-fire's ruddy
    gleam ;

And I could see my master, beside the watch-fire's light.
His face was calm and earnest, his eye was clear and
bright.

"Oh! what," he said, reflecting, to his comrade by his
side,
"Will they think home in England if we lose to-morrow's
ride?'
"We can but try our hardest!" the other said in turn ;
"The men have pluck and spirit, 'tis easy to discern."

And then, with the morning waking, we saw the gathering
force
Of the dark-faced Indian tribesmen, both skirmishers and
horse :
We saw them on the mountain, we saw them in the glen ;
We knew we had to reckon with dashing, daring men.

How still my master sat me ; how firm his seat and hand :
How cool and calm his orders to his gallant fighting
band.
And up the glen we saw them, the dark-faced warriors
stood,
Possessed of a strong position, and thirsting for our blood.

Then came the stirring order that made the pulses beat.
"Trot !—gallop !—*charge ! !*" the Colonel cried, and turned
round in his seat.

And faster still and faster, and up the glen we flew ;
With a shout at the squadron leaders, the Colonel led u-
    through.

Oh, how we hacked and hewed them, and how they fought
    and fell,
Those dark-faced Indian warriors, that stood so long and
    well ;
But we took the position, and routed them all at last ;
The dark-faced Indian warriors found that their lot was
    cast.

And so, three cheers for England ! There's life in England
    yet ;
The good old order changeth not when brave men's minds
    are set.
On one true-hearted purpose, and one true-hearted cause.
Of pure and wholesome government, and firm unbiassed
    laws.

And is there not a touch of love in good old England
    still,
That binds true hearts together, and makes men do her
    will ?
In spite of strikes and tumults, and smouldering discon-
    tent,
There's something left in England which only finds a
    vent

E

When troubles come, and then we find men who are glad
    to die
To save the name of England with fervent constancy ;
But look !—here comes the master, he loves this English
    farm.
His young wife walks beside him, and leans upon his
    arm.

Don't gallop off, you stupid, and look so wild and scared.
Come closer and be patted : there's nothing to be feared.
Stand still—yes, there—that's better, and let them stroke
    your nose ;
There's nothing to be frightened at in men in Sunday
    clothes.

MAJOR GEORGE WHYTE-MELVILLE.

† WHYTE-MELVILLE.

THURSDAY, DECEMBER 5th. 1878.

Poet and sportsman and scholar, we greet you —
    Shade of the past, still you move by our side ;
Still by the verge of the woodland we meet you,
    Waiting, and watching, and willing to ride.

Still. it would seem, in the gallop you cheer us,
    Sailing away over fallow and mead ;
Out in the open your spirit is near us,
    Moving the rider and stirring the steed.

Nor is this all, for your function is ever
    Still to lead those who are scribes of the chase,
Still to add zest to their effort, and never
    To fill them with thoughts which degrade or debase.

Help us to read in the pastime we treasure
    Something that raises mankind as we write,
Something above a mere craving for pleasure ;
    Shade of Whyte-Melville, still lead us aright.

Help us to find in the soul-stirring chorus,
    Which rings through the woodland and floats to the sky.
Something that brightens the pathway before us ;
    Spirit of friendship, still stir us to try.

Help us to cherish the chivalrous feeling
    That binds every sportsman who holds with the chase ;
Kindling his heart with affection, and healing
    Sores that are often so hard to erase.

So may we raise sporting literature, using
    Still the same efforts that brought you success ;
Humbly embodying your work, and infusing
    Some of your art amid those we address.

Lead us, then, Shade of the memory we cherish ;
   Lead, and we follow you still to the end.
Sport will not die, nor will chivalry perish,
   While every true sportsman is counted a friend.

NOVEMBER.

† NOVEMBER.

WELCOME the chase, with its balmy November !
   Welcome the colours of scarlet and grey !
Welcome the friends that we meet and remember,
   Year after year, on the opening day !

Blame me not, reader, nor say I'm romancing :
   Phantom-shaped horsemen I seem to discern,
Riding among the gay squadrons advancing,
   Each one equipped for the chase in his turn.

Close by the side of each sportsman is riding
   The shade of some friend who has loved him in chase,
Rousing him, helping him, stirring, and guiding
   The hunter who bears him with mettle and pace.

There down in Leicestershire, silently sailing,
   Assheton Smith flies o'er the fields of the Quorn,
Tackling the double and topping the railing,
   Gliding along to the sound of the horn.

Loatland's fair covert shows Goodall intently
   Watching the entry he bred with such care ;
"Gently, my bonny lads ; gently hounds, GENTLY !"
   Mystical whispers are stirring the air.

Newsman and Rhymer are gracefully speeding
   Over the ploughs of the Oakley to day,
Guiding their sons, who are true to their breeding,
   Stooping and driving and streaming away.

Lead us, O shades of true sportsmen departed !
   Move us to gallop and rouse us to ride ;
Bind us in friendship sincere and true-hearted,
   Phantoms of sportsmen still ride by our side.

Speak to us still when the horn and the holloa
   Ring through the woodland and rise to the sky :
Speak in the notes of the hounds that we follow,
   Crashing together and scouring to cry.

Speak, and let every good sportsman remember
    Hunting is based on good fellowship still ;
So let us welcome the month of November
    While it vouchsafes us good sport and goodwill.

Lead us, O shades of the memories we cherish !
    Lead us and lend us your mystical aid ;
Sport at its best will not dwindle or perish
    Under the care of the phantom brigade.

LORD WORCESTER.

† THE HUNTSMAN IN GREEN.

A SPORTSMAN I'll give you, a gentleman born,
    A man to be noted when seen :
The soul-stirring notes of his musical horn
Fall sweet to the ear and awaken the morn -
    Lord Worcester, the huntsman in green.

I've seen him on " Beckford," the flea-bitten grey,
  A hunter both gallant and keen ;
The old horse's spirit has drifted away,
But the rider remains, and is game to this day
  Lord Worcester, the huntsman in green.

He is seen at his best on the side of a gale,
  He knows where his quarry has been ;
When scent is both catchy and bad, and hounds fail
To own it, he shows them each turn in the vale —
  They trust him, this huntsman in green.

They've a character, too, have these beautiful hounds,
  Their necks are both graceful and lean ;
How handy they seem, ever kept within bounds,
From the heart of the wood their sweet music resounds,
  And the cheer of the huntsman in green.

There's a whistle away, and a cap in the air,
  But never a fuss or a scene ;
The buff and blue squadron intend to be *there* —
Those men who can ride, and those ladies so fair,
  Who follow the huntsman in green.

And over the open they race and they ride,
  Till the fox by the hedgerow is seen ;
The huntsman's big hunter makes use of his stride,
And those who are leading the galloping tide
  Hear " Who-whoop ! " from the huntsman in green.

The crowd has gone home, and Lord Worcester is still
  As keen as a lad of fourteen ;
See, the sunlight is dim on the opposite hill,
But he walks a good fox to his death with a will—
  He's a huntsman, this huntsman in green.

THE FOX BY THE HEDGEROW IS SEEN.

And home is the word ; there's a smile on his face,
  It tells of contentment I ween ;
He has shown us a gallop and handled a brace,
But it's what we expect, and it's often the case,
  With the Badminton huntsman in green.

Sess, sess, brother sportsman, go home and lie down,
  Take your soup and clear out the tureen ;
Sess, sess, brother sportsman, go home and lie down,
  Long, long may you lead us in chase with renown,
    Still known as the huntsman in green !

WHO-WHOOP! IT'S A KILL.

† JOHN HARGREAVES.[1]

I'LL give you a sportsman of Dorsetshire fame,
A nailer to gallop and ride ;
Through the rough and the smooth he is always the same,
For he's always in front of his field ; and his name
Is one Berkshire men speak of with pride.

And once when I saw him, a January day,
'Twas at Bradford plantation we found,
And a hat in the air and a holloa away
Brought a thrill to the crowd, who were happy and gay,
And the soul-stirring note of a hound.

[1] Master and Huntsman of the Cattistock Foxhounds.

And forrard again, ever crossing the breeze,
The fox is still forward, I ween.
See, the good hounds are speeding away by the trees
With the Master beside them still going at ease
To note where their quarry has been.

But mark, on the fallow the hounds are at fault,
Like beagles they stoop and they try ;
But the Master's " Hold hard ! " brings the field to a halt,
For he holds that a sportsman is not worth his salt
Who presses hounds scouring to cry.

And forrard again ; how he twists and he turns
This fox, yet he leads us a dance ;
But the Master is hard on his track and soon learns
His movements, which movements he quickly discerns :
No doubt he could hunt him to France.

We sink to the valley, and rise to the hill,
To old maiden castle we fly ;
The earth is unstopped—will he gain it ?   He will !
No ! Look !   they have got him. " Who-whoop ! " it's a kill.
" Who-whoop ! then, who-whoop ! " is the cry.

And journeying homewards we think of the day,
The whips and the huntsman so keen ;
We think of the crowd ever streaming away
O'er the hills of the Cattistock, so bright and so gay.
And ponder on what we have seen.

So here's to John Hargreaves ! long may he survive,
With still the same story to tell ;
In the heat of the chase may he always contrive
To ride up to his hounds, with their dash and their drive.
In the country he governs so well.

THE OLD MARE'S STORY.

† THE OLD MARE'S STORY.

AND you are the hack pensioned off by your master.
Ah, yes. I remember, he lived in the vale ;
A friend of our house—yes, that was a disaster :
He fractured his thigh coming over the rail.

And I !   If you wish it I'll tell you my story ;
But look at the foal I have bred, see him pass.
His father's career was a record of glory
In racing ; see there ! how he moves on the grass.

My mistress, the wife of my master, you know her,
As good as an angel, as bright as the day.
No horse that was bred could disturb her or throw her,
How gamely she rode when the hounds were away.

Well, when she was younger her parents insisted
On making a match with a low, drinking peer.
She loathed him, poor girl, and stood out and resisted :
But no, it was useless, he filled her with fear.

My master, the man she loved dearly, was frantic,
And swore a round oath he would bear her away.
We lived at the time by the mighty Atlantic,
Where leagues of bright sand made a fringe to the bay.

And weird was the night, while the moonlight was falling,
Across the grey waters, so silent and still.
And weird was the way where the seagull was calling
His mate from the cavern, down under the hill.

But hush ! see the face at the window appearing
All hooded and veiled : " Are you ready ?   Then spring.
My darling ! my darling ! " and soon we're careering
Along the bright sands with a stride and a swing.

I

And I !   Yes, I feel it, their true hearts are beating
In time to the strokes of my stride as I fly.
Her arms are around him, I hear the sweet greeting
He gives her, and know there's a light in his eye.

Ten miles ! they are light, and the sands are good riding ;
But still, it's an effort with two on your back.
On, onward we go, and on, on we are striding,
The blood of old Stockwell still tells on the track.

On, on, yes, I know it, their lives are depending
On me, the dumb steed, I'll be true to the end.
I'll make a game effort. I know I'm defending
The right ; yes, at least I'll be counted a friend.

On, on to the hamlet, the grey dawn is breaking
O'er the church where the marriage is quietly read.
The good ship is anchored, e'en now she is shaking
Her sails to the breeze that springs up overhead.

Away o'er the waters the good ship is sailing,
Away from a lifetime of trouble and care.
See now ! how the sailors are grouped—they are hailing
" Three cheers for the chestnut, three cheers for the mare."

And now I have told you the whole of my story
I'm glad you are pleased, it is pleasant to tell.
There's a touch of romance and a flavour of glory,
But here comes the man with the corn, through the dell.

THE IRISH DEALER AND THE OLD LADY.

† THE IRISH HORSEDEALER AND THE OLD LADY.

Ah, good mornin' to ye, madam ! it's yourself I'm glad to
  meet,

An' the three young ladies with ye—tear an' ages, it's a
  treat ;

It's a horse they said ye wanted, faix I heard it in the
  town,

So I've brought the one to suit ye · there's a colour, rich
  and brown !

When ye take him up to London, he'll be handy for the
    Row,
An' the ladies there will ride him—ah, bedad, they'll make
    a show !
It's a husband each he'll find them : dukes, bedad, and
    nothing less,
An' you'll bless the Irish dealer for his forethought, an'
    confess

It was all the horse that did it, och, you'll say he's just the
    man ;
Then you'll praise me to the chaperons, an' they'll all adopt
    the plan.
Ah, now, ladies, don't be smilin', it's yourselves that
    understand
How to captivate the bachelors an' take the proffered
    hand.

An' it's madam there was young herself, an' beautiful as well—
But we'll change the conversation, it's the horse I've
    brought to sell ;
What's the price ? He's worth a hundred, but I'm anxious to
    be kind,
So I'll just take sixty guineas, an' he's cheap at that you'll
    find.

Run him down the road now, Patrick. Woa ! now stand
    him there awhile ;
Mark his head so nate an' clever : there is action, too, an'
    style.

Whisht, now whisht ! I'll tell a secret, it's me wife that
  likes the horse,
For she drives to church on Sundays with the children ;
  but of course

Av the ladies really want him, faix, I'll try what I can do :
But she'll feel his loss severely, an' the boys will miss him
  too.
So you'll give the price I ask, ma'am. Well, I'm plazed
  we've made a deal ;
Arrah ! now, you've bought a treasure, it's a fact I'll not
  conceal.

Well, good mornin' to you, ladies, sure I hope we'll meet
  again ;
I'm goin' back to poor ould Oirland ; but at that I'll not
  complain,
For they pays no rint in Oirland, an' can sell the horses
  cheap ;
Yes, I'll mind the step. Good day, ma'am : faix, you're
  right, it's rather steep.

THE PRIEST AND THE VOTER.

* THE PRIEST AND THE VOTER.

FATHER WALSH was here last night, bedad, the Priest, you
    know, from town,
Yes, he came to see me, Patrick, on his cob, the dappled
    brown ;
" 'Tis your vote I'm wantin', Larry," said the Priest, " it's
    what I wrote
In my letter to ye, Larry, it's me man that wants your
    vote."

" Ah !" I said, " I think I'm changin', me digestion is so
    queer,
It's home rule that makes me head ache, not the whisky,
    never fear."

" You're a haythen baste," the Father said, " I hope you'l
    be forgiven,
But there's evil times in store for ye, ye'll never go to
    heaven."

Then the Priest he looked again and saw me wink the other
    eye,
" It's yourself that's laughin', Larry, faix I think you'd
    better cry,
For the man who will not vote me way I'll turn into a rat,
So just think before ye vex me, just be careful what ye're at.

" It's the saints that help me, Larry, at election times, ye
    see,
An' its funny things they do sometimes to save the ould
    country."
" By the powers, I'm glad ye've tould me, Father Walsh,"
    I said to him,
" There's an ould brown cat my wife has got at home, we
    call him Jim,

" An' it's rats he's mighty partial to, I'll shut him up, bedad,
For I'd not like Jim to eat me, arrah now, that would be
    bad."
" Ye're an unbelavin' sinner," said the Priest, " that's what
    ye are,
'Tis the saints that kill bad men like you, now don't ye go
    too far."

"An' may be ye'll read the funeral, Father, darlin'," I
 replied.

"There's a churchyard on the hill now, you can see from
 far an' wide,

It's the healthiest churchyard onywhere, a most convanient
 place,

So just tell the saints to lave me there, and just explain
 the case."

Then the Priest became persuasive, "Ah ! now, Larry, don't
 ye think

Ye would like a quiet talk, me boy, may be ye'd like a
 drink.

Take the flask now, Larry, help yourself, I'm sure ye'd
 like a pull."

"Whisht !" I said, "it's what I'll do, bedad, I see you've
 filled it full.

"When we get a home rule parliament, now, Father dear,
 confess,

We'll get whisky sould for nothin', yes, an' spirits bought
 for less."

"To be sure ye will," the Father said, "the laws will be
 sublime.

Are there other things ye'd like, me boy ? Just speak, for
 now's your time."

"'Tis me corduroys is shabby, Father darlin', they're a pair
That was bought for William Rufus when he came to
 Cahirmee fair,

An' the sate is hardly dacent, but I wear my coat tails
   long,

For I'm bashful, Father darlin', though I look so tall and
   strong."

"Every boy shall have two pair a-piece," the Father then
   replied.

"Faix now, Larry, you have never known an Irish Priest
   that lied?"

"Devil a one," I said, "'twould spoil the game entirely,
   don't you see,

For their prayers would all be humbug without truth and
   purity."

An' with that he looked uncomfortable, "Ah, Larry, then,"
   he said,

"We'll depend upon your vote, me man," and stroked me
   on the head.

"Now about them breeches, Father, faix I doubt their being
   supplied,

When the members meet at College Green, they'll be so
   occupied

"In bating out each other's brains, that we'll be left out i'
   the could,

An' they'll tear the buttons off the brecks, they're funny
   boys, I'm tould."

"Whisht! now, Larry, don't belave it," said the Father,
   "they're genteel,

An' they'll live like doves together, for their nature is to heal."

" Ah, no, Father, no, I'm changin', it's me system's all awry.
Faix them Salisbury boys is dacent chaps, we'll let them
    have a try."
" Ye're a hard benighted crayture," said the Priest, " the
    saints will come
Rather hard upon ye, Larry, an' a curse upon your home.

" 'Tis a rat they'll turn ye into, Larry ; Larry, that they will."
" Faix," I said, " it's what I'd like, bedad, there's one down
    at the mill
That has got a situation that would suit me to the ground,
He's the run of all the provender, with board an' lodgin'
    found."

Then he went his way blasphemin' me, I heard him all the
    way,
But I have not grown a rat's tail yet ; there's time, bedad, I
    may !
Ah ! now, Patrick, we'll be practical, just for a change we will,
An' we'll stick to poor ould Oirland, boys, to poor ould
    Oirland still.

THE IRISH CARMAN.

* THE IRISH CARMAN.

An! now, Capt'in, yes, I'll drive ye round the Phœnix and
    the town,
An' I'll show ye Dublin city, it's a place of much renown :
Av ye like to sit ajacent, sure it's four the car contains,
But it's six can sit familiar. Whisht ! now Pat, hand up the
    reins.

Hand them up now, help the ladies.   Och ! be gentle with
    them, Pat,
Ah ! don't blush now, I can see the colour rising through
    your hat.

t's the quality we've got to-day, be jabers ! an' I'm proud :
.et me whisper to ye, Capt'in, which one is it?   not too
     loud.

Ah ! now, Capt'in, don't be laughin', I'm a married man,
     don't mind
Trustin' Paddy with a secret, it's a heart he has, an' kind.
Look ! here comes the Lord Lieutenant, here's Cadogan,
     here's the man,
It's himself that always winks at me an' shakes hands when
     he can.

But to-day he's mighty bashful, it's the ladies make him
     shy,
You can see his modest nature in the corner of his eye ;
There's a lady on the pavement there was at the ball last
     night ;
An' her dress it was a low one, green, bedad ! trimmed up
     with white.

'Twas her partner from the barracks slithered a pink ice
     down her back,
" Och ! " she said, " it's mighty could it is, I think it seems
     to lack
Just a trifle of the flavour which is pleasant to the taste,
An' it's like the polar regions come to settle round me
     waist."

Och ! now, Capt'in, faix, the twenty-ninth of February falls
    to-day,

'Twill be eight long years before we see this day twelve
    month they say ;

But it's leap year, Capt'in darlin', and the girls will have a
    chance,

For they'll ax the men to marry them, bedad ! that will
    enhance

Every well arranged flirtation ; don't be anxious, Capt'in
    dear,

They'll be winkin' at ye, Capt'in, they'll be at ye, never
    fear :

But we'll change the conversation, for I see the ladies ken

What I mane, bedad ! they're laughin'. Ah ! they're hard
    upon the men.

You'll stay out a little longer ? Yes, av course ye will,
    an' go

By the other road, yer honour ; is it home we'll drive an'
    slow ?

There's a mighty hole somewhere abouts, the work is not
    complete ;

Ah ! hould up, ye baste, don't tumble down, there's ladies
    on the seat.

Tear an' ages, man, we're in it, it's the wheel that's breakin'
    now,

An' the car is turnin' over Whisht ! be jabers, here's a row.

Lift the ladies up now, Capt'in, seat them there upon the
    bank.
Arrah ! now, there's no one hurt at all, the mare has
    touched her flank.

Well, it's pleasant conversation an' divarsion we have had,
An' a rale ould smash, begorra, it's the shafts is broke,
    bedad !
Well, good mornin' to ye, Capt'in, faix ! the hole it was to
    blame ;
Och ! be jabers, I've enjoyed myself, I hope ye've done the
    same.

THE IRISH INN.

*THE IRISH INN.

[The following represents a conversation between the landlord of an Irish Inn in the wilds of Ireland, where rough and indifferent shooting can be obtained, and a sportsman, whose custom he is anxious to secure as a shooting tenant.]

Ony game, sor? Sure they're teeming,
Ye can see the feathers gleaming
In the sunlight when you're standing yonder by the ould shebeen.
Rabbits? Och! the ground is crawling,
It's yourself that will be falling,
Faix! they run between your ankles thick as grass upon the green.

Hares?   Be jabers! an' there's plenty,
Faix! when I was four and twenty
I could never grow the number of their namesakes on my
   head;
   An' the snipe, you'll see them rising
   In a way that's most surprising,
May the divil fly away with them that doubt what I have
   said.

Lions?   How strange you should be asking,
   There were three great lions basking
In the garden by the sundial when I went to milk the cow.
   Ah! now, Major, don't be winking,
   'Tis myself you'd chaff, I'm thinking:
Well, I see you like romancing, so I'm right there, anyhow.

   Sure it's quite at home you'll feel, sor,
   For we're always most genteel, sor,
And we keep the highest company that's found in ony land:
   All the guests are influential,
   Whisht! now, I'll be confidential,   .
'Twas the Queen, she wrote a letter with her own most
   gracious hand:

   " Mister Murphy, you're the man, sor,
   An' you'll help me if you can, sor,"
Said the Queen in her epistle, " Mister Murphy, you're the
   man.

All my three sons want a change, now,
You've a lovely mountain range, now,
Sure the air would brace them, Murphy, try an' take them
av you can."

So I wrote, " It's what I'll do, ma'am,
Av it's for the likes of you, ma'am,
Is there any kind of diet that yourself would recommend ? "
" Asses' milk is very healthy,"
Wrote the Queen, "I'm very wealthy,
An' I'll pay for ony extras for themselves or for a friend."

" Faix ! " I wrote, " we'll not deny them,
It's the cow that shall supply them,"
So an aide-de-camp from Windsor was sent over with the
pails ;
Mixed with rum 'twas just the thing, sor,
An' it made them dance an' sing, sor :
" Ah ! " they said, " long life to Murphy, his invention
never fails."

Av ye lead a single life, sor,
An' you're seeking for a wife, sor,
I can find one for you, Major, an' I'll trate you as a friend :
Av I can't, why it's a pity,
All the girls in Dublin city
Say that Murphy finds them husbands and on Murphy they
depend.

There are six substantial daughters,
I can take you to their quarters,
Oh ! their skins are soft an' pleasant, for I've stroked them
with my hand ;
You will find them all a catch, sor,
I could bring about the match, sor,
For ye see I've tact an' manners, an' I'd act at your
command.

Well, I'm glad to see you smile, sor,
An' you think it's worth your while, sor,
Faix ! I've shown you the advantages we give you at the
Inn ;
An' ye like my bit of blarney,
Divil a one in ould Killarney,
Where they bred me, but was buried in his coffin with a
grin.

So you think you'd like to stay, sor,
Faix ! We'll make you blithe and gay, sor,
It's myself that's so persuasive and my failings are but
small ;
Av you'd like to take a walk, sor,
Or a confidential talk, sor,
Why, just call out Mister Murphy, an' I'll hear you through
the wall.

IRISH DEALER AND WRONG CUSTOMER.

* THE IRISH HORSEDEALER AND THE WRONG CUSTOMER.

An' bedad !   I'm glad I've met you,
For you see I don't forget you,
Sure I've brought the horse from Oirland for yer honour by
the ship ;
He was bred in ould Kilkenny,
An' I'll lay yer my last penny
That he'll go from night till morning without asking for the
whip.

Tired ! No ; the man who sould him
Said you've only got to hould him
An' he'd wear your breeches threadbare ere he'd ask you
    for a halt.
Come, sir, take him an' be lanient,
You can pay me when convanient,
Them that's bred and reared in England never will be
    worth their salt.

'Twas the blind man saw him walking,
An' the dumb man started talking
When he passed me, an' he tould me he was worth his
    weight in gould.
" Whisht ! " the deaf man said, " you're joking,
I can hear the fun you're poking,
Sure the eighty Irish members could not buy him, so I'm
    tould."

'Twas last week in Dublin city —
Don't ye know it ?   More's the pity —
Well, I lunched with Mister Morley off a leg of roasted
    pork ;
He was on his best behaviour,
An' he begged me as a favour
Av I'd spare him half an hour for a confidential talk.

" Pat," he said, " you know my feelings,
How I tries for pleasant dealings
With the boys that form the Cabinet there in mighty
    London town,

Arrah ! now, I'll not evict you,
An' I'll see they don't convict you
When you're short of rint next quarter, av you'll let me
    buy the brown.

    " For, ye see, there's Asquith seeking
    For a nag, I heard him speaking
To his wife about a hunter down at Spencer's in the shires,
    An' I thought I might present it
    From myself, you'll not repent it,
For they're dacent kind of people, an' it's blood that she
    requires.

    "An' besides, there's many measures
    That the Liberal Party treasures,
Av the boys will pull together we shall prosper in the end ;
    So I ask for your assistance,
    An' we will not mind resistance,
Pat," he spoke with great emotion, "you will not refuse a
    friend."

    "Mister Morley," I repeated,
    "Don't get up," I said, "be seated,
Is the case so very pressing?" "Divil a lie," said honest
    John ;
    Then I said yer honour'd buy him,
    "Well," he said. "then let him try him,
Av he don't, then I must have him, but ye must not keep
    me long."

What !   The horse belonged to you, sor?
An' my statements are not true, sor?
He was bred down here in Wiltshire an' ye know the very
    farm?
Lame behind, and cribs and whistles?
Is not worth a feed of thistles?
Well, ye see, sor, it's this way, sor, now I'll tell ye ; pray be
    calm.

Now, my father was a man, sor—
Av ye doubt my word, ye can, sor —
With a janius for invention, an' my mother was the same :
So ye see it's handed down, sor,
An' has brought us much renown, sor,
Like our ancestors before us an' the stock from whence we
    came.

Arrah ! now, yer honour's laughing,
Faix ! I see you're fond of chaffing,
It's the smile that makes us handsome, an' I see ye know
    the way.
Well, I'm mighty plazed we've met, sor,
It's yourself I'll not forget, sor.
Shake my hand; good afternoon, sor, we will deal another
    day.

February, 1895.

THE BOY ON THE PONY.

* THE BOY ON THE PONY.

THE boy on the pony, who sits so serenely?
Ah! well you may ask.   You are strange to the shire?
Anon when we find he will show you how keenly
He rides o'er the vale, this young son of the squire.

He lives at the Hall with his father and mother:
His nurse cannot make him look tidy, they say;
His hat is forlorn, he won't wear any other,
His breeks have been ragged for many a day.

See the huge piece of cake he is quietly eating,
  Held up with both hands—he is friends with the cook :
Look, now, as he sits at his ease, he is treating
  The hounds to a morsel ; how wistful they look.

Last month, on a balmy bright day in November,
  We found in the woodlands and ran to the vale :
The boy on the pony was there, I remember,
  Both covered with mud from the head to the tail.

The country was cramped, but the pony was clever,
  The ditch in the meadow, the drop in the field,
He had them in turn ; I assure you he never
  Made half a mistake, and he never would yield.

We ran for three hours where the country was deepish,
  The field was diminished, the leaders were blown ;
And many a good rider went home and looked sheepish,
  But the boy on the pony was holding his own.

At last, when our fox was dead beat and before us,
  We came to a fence that made all of us stop ;
We heard the good hounds and their modified chorus,
  We looked at the fence, and we thought of the drop.

There was only one place, that was narrow and trappy,
  Beneath a tall tree, where a horse could not pass ;
But the boy on the pony crept through. Oh ! how happy
  He looked as they landed all safe on the grass.

Three fields further on they ran into their quarry,
  The boy on the pony was with them alone.
Who-whoop ! the delight of the huntsman and Harry,
  The whip, whose good hunter was beaten and done.

They said that at night he came home, and returning
  Found his new French governess boiling with rage ;
He'd cut all his work, for he thought the best learning
  For him was Diana's adventurous page.

And when the young culprit was brought to his mother,
  A fair lady rider who came from Kildare,
She fell on his neck and declared that no other
  Young hopeful alive with her son could compare.

The brush in due course was well mounted ; his father
  Still points to the trophy, it hangs on the wall ;
He smiles as he shows it, some say he would rather
  Lose everything else that he owns at the Hall.

We toasted the boy, with all honour and glory,
  That night through the length and the breadth of the shire.
So now I have told you the whole of the story
  Of this foxhunting son of the foxhunting squire.

But, look ! they are off and are drawing the spinney ;
  You'll see our best country, I'm glad you are here.
They'll run, I feel sure ; there's a scent, for a guinea.
  Tally ho ! he's away ; follow on to the cheer.

THE SHADE OF THE HUNTSMAN.

* THE SHADE OF THE HUNTSMAN.

Why, yes, I'm the farmer ; yes, that is my calling,
  And you are the gent that has come to the Grange.
Come in, sir, come in, sir, the snow is appalling.
  Not wet ?   If you are I can lend you a change.

Well, what shall it be ; there is whisky and brandy,
  There's fine home brewed ale, and a cake and a cheese.
There's a cut of cold roast and there's other things handy.
  Come in, sir, you're welcome ; sit down at your ease.

Why, yes, if you wish, I will tell you the story
  Of the shade of the huntsman who died in the chase ;
But, ere we begin, here's a health to his glory :
  How well I recall his intelligent face.

Poor Joe, we were friends, yes, our hearts were united,
  I knew him from childhood, a broth of a boy ;
He'd the run of the house and he came uninvited,
  And welcome, the children received him with joy.

His hounds were perfection, so sorty and clever,
  Such neat necks and shoulders and bone to the feet,
With hearts that could last, they could gallop for ever ;
  To see them in chase was a sight and a treat.

So quick at their work, they were true to their breeding,
  They'd race to his holloa and fly to his cheer ;
How quickly he spotted the hound that was leading,
  His eye on the pack as he rode in the rear.

One day when we hunted, one balmy November,
  We found in the woodlands and ran to the vale,
We passed through this farm ; yes, how well I remember
  Joe sailing away over bullfinch and rail.

We came to the brook, Joe was at it and over,
  He showed us the way on the gallant grey mare,
And over the fallow and over the clover,
  The fences were tackled with plenty to spare.

And yonder he fell, where the shadows are falling
    From yonder tall oak tree, see, there on the grass :
So game to the last and so true to his calling,
    A man and a leader, a bad one to pass.

A rabbit hole broke the mare's leg as she landed,
    She crushed him completely, he died where he fell :
The hounds were at fault, they were turning right handed.
    Their fox was dead beat and was sinking the dell.

And still of a night, when the moonlight is stealing
    Across the dark ride of the woodland, they say
The shade of the huntsman is seen, ever feeling
    The reins as he handles the shade of the grey.

And still through the woodland you see the pack spreading,
    The shades of good hounds who have loved him in chase :
In front of their huntsman each phantom hound threading
    The covert with movements of exquisite grace.

And over the open still lashing and driving,
    The phantom-shaped pack ever gallantly fly ;
Each hound in his place, and the leaders contriving
    To keep up the pace, for the scent is breast high.

Beside them their huntsman, so gracefully sailing,
    Is watching their movements, still keen as of yore ;
The shade of the mare as she tops the high railing
    Still carries him onward, and well to the fore.

On, onward, they go, where the meadows are gleaming
   In silvery grandeur, and silent and still ;
Away by the brook, where the moonbeams are streaming,
   The phantom-shaped pack passes over the hill.

And weird is the scene over which they are speeding,
   And weird are the colours of silver and grey,
And weird are the hounds that are silently leading
   The ghost of the huntsman —still, forrard, away.

And still in the hunt there are those who maintain it,
   Unseen in the daylight he rides by your side,
And when you have got a good start and retain it,
   He moves you to gallop and stirs you to ride.

He stirs you to ride when your comrades are moving
   Around you in chase, ever true to the end :
He stirs you to ride when the moments are proving
   That every true sportsman is counted a friend.

Well, well, men may laugh and declare I'm romancing,
   For me 'tis enough, I care not what they say,
I know that at night when the moonbeams are dancing
   Poor Joe and the hounds are still streaming away.

Good night, sir, good night. Mind the step. How it's snowing.
   I'm glad you are pleased at the story I've told.
My word ! what a gale ! see the trees, how it's blowing
   The drifts must be deep over there on the wold.

THE RACE OF THE YEAR.

*THE RACE OF THE YEAR.

COMMON'S DERBY, 1891.

Come down to the Derby, come down to the race,
Come down to the downs with a smile on your face
In spite of the rain and the absence of sun,
There's something to see in Isonomy's son ;
You'll find some good fellows and lots of good cheer,
It's always the case at the race of the year.

A wonderful sight is this wonderful course
To all who profess a regard for the horse.

Just look at the crowd from the bend of the land,
Like bees in a swarm all about the grand stand.
The roar of the voices that falls on the ear
Has a wonderful sound at the race of the year.

You've plenty of choice if you look for a nag ;
See the blood-looking team come along with the drag.
Each horse, in his place as he faces the hill,
Breaks into a gallop and moves with a will.
The broken-down hunter tied up in the rear
Hears the sound of the horn at the race of the year.

But now to the paddock, the crowd is select,
Some come to be seen and some come to inspect
Two sons of St. Simon, two sons of Bend Or,
While Energy's offspring shows well to the fore ;
This Gouverneur fills us with feelings of fear,
Sent over from France for the race of the year.

There's something uncommon (forgive me the pun)
In Alington's [1] brown, good Isonomy's son ;
They've entered the horse in the baronet's name,
But both have a share in his fall or his fame ;
The favourite was bred by the Dorsetshire peer,
He looks like the nag for the race of the year.

[1] Common was the property of Lord Alington and Sir Frederic
Johnstone.

" They're off ! " at the fall of the flag, with a speed
That tries the condition of those in the lead.
They're off, in the teeth of the wind and the rain
That sweeps over Surrey's historical plain.
In passing the furzes it seems to be clear
The Deemster is out of the race of the year.

And after the Corner the shouting is loud
When Stirling's two grandsons come out of the crowd,
And Common and Gouverneur stealing away
Show the Birdcatcher line has a value to-day ;
But Common comes up as the multitude cheer,
And adds to his record the race of the year.

We're proud of the Derby, we're proud of the breed
Of horses that go with such wonderful speed ;
We're proud of the men who are honest and straight
In riding and racing and try to create
True sport, in the sense that is highest and dear
To England, whose pride is this race of the year.

OVER THE MOORLAND.

*OVER THE MOORLAND.[1]

[AT HAWKCOMBE HEAD WITH THE DEVON AND SOMERSET
STAGHOUNDS, FRIDAY, SEPT. 27, 1895.]

OVER the moorland, now gently, mare, gently,
  Anthony heads him away from the herd ;
All the field watch his direction intently,
  Over the moorland he flies like a bird.

[1] This poem came out in *The County Gentleman*, Oct. 5, 1895.

H

Brow, bay, and trey, see him pause on the heather,
  Standing majestically, game for a spring ;
Graceful in attitude, light as a feather,
  Bold as a lion, and proud as a king.

Over the moorland so easily stealing,
  Past the Doone Valley and Hoccombe away ;
On to the skyline, the good stag is feeling
  The breeze in his face, for he means it to-day.

Lay on the pack, they are eager and ready ;
  Quickly they own it and gamely they try ;
All the field waiting by Shepherd's Cot.   Steady !
  Over the moorland we gallantly fly.

Scouring to cry, see them lashing and driving.
  " Forrard, away ! " hark at Anthony's cheer.
Over the watercourse, every hound striving
  Hard for a place, while we ride in the rear.

Onward by Stoford the good stag is leading,
  At the weir water he stands in the stream.
Mark him at bay ; but his heart and his breeding
  Stand in good stead on the moor, it would seem.

Over the moorland, still onward we press him,
  Through Culbone Plantation he sinks to the sea :
And though we are eager to kill him we bless him,
  This king of the forest, so fearless and free.

Down through the woodland the secretary slots him .
    Hark ! there's a note of a hound from the rear.
Into the Severn sea somebody spots him -
    Cheer them on, Anthony !   Anthony, cheer !

A boat is at hand ; he is lassoed and taken,
    Taken and killed : many horses are done :
Many a good rider and steed have forsaken
    The chase for to-day, and are out of the run.

Luck and long life to the hunt and the Master,
    Long may we hunt the wild stag in the chase
Over wild Exmoor, and free from disaster,
    With horses and hounds that can gallop and race.

Over the moorland the bright moon is sailing,
    Over the scene of the chase of the deer ;
Still in my slumbers the good stag is failing—
    Cheer them on, Anthony !   Anthony, cheer !

HOUNDS AT HORSE EXERCISE.

* HOUNDS AT HORSE EXERCISE.

ALL the yellow corn is waving,
And the harvester is saving
All the field of golden barley with the old horse and the
grey;
See the pack are game and sprightly,
Oh! they tread the road so lightly,
I can hear the rustling music of their feet upon the way.

All the singing birds are singing,
And the bits are lightly ringing,
And the horses beat the measure, making music as we ride;

See, the chestnut's veins are swelling
On her neck, her blood is telling
As she bears me on the journey with her long and swinging
stride.

Oh ! the hounds are fit and jolly
As we jog them by the folly,
Oh ! they love an outing, bless you, for it makes them
bright and gay.
O'er each wistful face uplifted,
Thoughts of sport have sweetly drifted,
And I hear the rustling music of their feet upon the way.

Till the end I shall remember
These bright mornings in September,
With the silver river running with its heaps of drifting weed :
In the sky the clouds are racing,
And below the lights are chasing
Every shadow in succession as it glides across the mead.

And the music of the morning
Floats along the golden awning
That is forming as the sunlight spreads and strengthens
into day ;
And the sounds of nature mingle
With the hounds, my senses tingle
As I hear the rustling music of their feet upon the way.

All the countryside is ringing,
And the singing birds are singing,

And the voices of the morning strike across the silver air :
    Nature cheers us, while she reaches
    All our better thoughts, and teaches
Men to love her, for her influence is ever bright and fair.

    Nature comes as a refiner :
    To mankind the Great Designer
Speaks in language sweet and solemn through the voices of
    the day :
    All my better heart rejoices
    As I hear those mystic voices
And, again, the rustling music of the hounds upon the way.

    I can see the sunlight streaming
    Where the water meads are gleaming,
And the landscape in its grandeur spreads around me far
    and wide ;
    There the village smoke is lifting
    Where the clouds are lightly drifting,
And I look on smiling England and my soul is filled with
    pride.

    Turn again, my lads, retracing
    All our steps, the breeze is bracing,
Still the horses beat the measure, making music bright and
    gay :
    See, the hounds are game and sprightly,
    As they tread the ground so lightly
I can hear the rustling music of their feet upon the way.

THE SISTERS ARE SCOURING TO CRY.

*THE SISTERS ARE SCOURING¹ TO CRY;

OR,

A DAY WITH FREEMAN AND THE LADY PACK OF THE SOUTH AND WEST WILTS FOXHOUNDS.

SIT down in your saddle, they mean it to-day,
  The huntsman is cheering—"Yut try - y !"
There's a cap in the air and it's forrard away !
And all the men's faces are happy and gay,
  For the sisters are scouring to cry.

¹ This word is pronounced "scoring" in the language of the chase.

They can hunt on the fallow and run on the grass,
   They can stoop, they can drive, they can fly.
Hold hard for a moment ! Now let the pack pass ;
If your hunter be slow you will find it a farce
   When the sisters are scouring to cry.

Out over the downs they are steady from hare ;
   They'll let a round dozen go by.
How quickly they drive the good fox from his lair,
He says to himself, " It's a case of beware
   When the sisters are scouring to cry."

Away and away, they are sinking the vale,
   Each hound like a bird in the sky,
And Freeman is marking their work as they sail,
While all of us know we must keep within hail
   When the sisters are scouring to cry.

See Martin, the master, so quick and so keen,
   A horseman whom none can defy ;
His hands are perfection, his seat is serene,
It's a very big fence that can stop him, I ween,
   When the sisters are scouring to cry.

We stand by the earths where the fox goes to ground,
   The fox that made everyone fly ;
We look in the face of each musical hound,
How level they look— there is time to look round—
   How level when scouring to cry.

The moonbeams are falling—I slumber again,
  And Freeman is cheering—" Vut try—y !"
But hark ! He's away ! Am I riding in vain ?
The roll of the gallop sweeps over the plain,
  And the sisters are scouring to cry.

March. 1895.

THE STRANGER FROM TOWN.

* THE STRANGER FROM TOWN
ON THE BLOOD-LOOKING BAY.

WE met at the village, two hundred and more,
The local men thought there was pleasure in store,
And everyone talked, with a smile on his face,
Of records and deeds of the men of the chase :
But one was unknown in that brilliant array—
A stranger from town on a blood-looking bay.

How everyone turned and took stock of the steed,
Almost thoroughbred, and so true to his breed ;
A head that was gentle, and generous, and kind,
Such strength in the back and such quarters behind.
They said at the meet, " He'll be sailing away,
This stranger from town on the blood-looking bay."

And after the hunter they looked at the man :
" A picture," they said ; " find a fault if you can.
A gentleman born, it is easy to trace
The best of blue blood in his features and face."
But quiet withal, he had little to say,
The stranger from town on the blood-looking bay.

We found in the gorse, I will give you my word,
He jumped the big gate that was locked like a bird :
Through the best of the vale he went sailing along,
The fences were stiff, and the scent it was strong.
There were two in the van : one, a man on a grey,
And the stranger from town on the blood-looking bay.

Still plainly I see them, these two in the van,
Each rode with a will and each rode like a man :
And one was well known and was always in front,
The pick of the country, the pride of the hunt :
But there soon came a time when he had to give way
To the stranger from town on the blood-looking bay.

How gamely he rode and how gamely the horse
Took fences and rails as they came in his course ;
And many a good hunter was beaten and blown
When the stranger was forward and holding his own.
We knew he had one who could gallop and stay,
The stranger from town on the blood-looking bay.

The run of the season for distance and pace,
An hour and a half, and a regular race.
The stranger it was took the fox from the hounds,
Who bayed at their quarry with musical sounds ;
And no one compared in that brilliant array
With the stranger from town on the blood-looking bay.

And who the man was is a mystery still,
This stranger who led us, and rode with a will.
We heard that he only came down by the train ;
We all of us hoped we might meet him again ;
And we talk of the rider and horse to this day,
The stranger from town on the blood-looking bay.

PRINTED BY
SPOTTISWOODE AND CO., NEW-STREET SQUARE
LONDON